Puppets

Julie Haydon

Contents

Chapter 1

In a Play

These people are **actors** in a **play**.
They are standing on a stage.

2

This is a puppet play.
There are no people in this play.
The puppets are on a stage too.

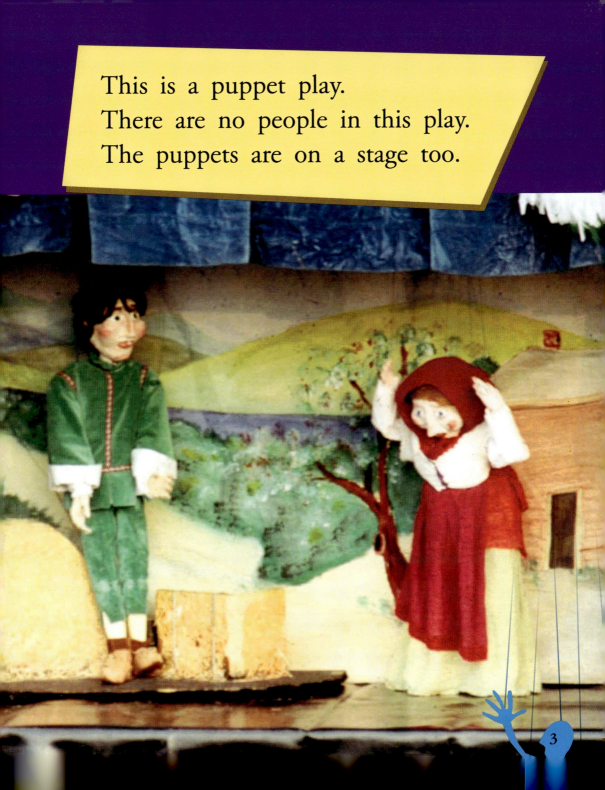

Chapter 2

Making Puppets Move

People make puppets move.
The people who make puppets move
are called **puppeteers**.

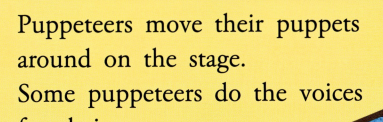

Puppeteers move their puppets
around on the stage.
Some puppeteers do the voices
for their puppets too.

5

Sometimes puppeteers stand on the stage with their puppets.
The puppeteers wear black clothes so they are hard to see.

Sometimes puppeteers hide behind the stage.

7

Chapter 3

About Puppets

There are many kinds of puppets.
Puppets can be made from lots of things.

these puppets are made from card

this puppet is made from wood and cloth

8

You can see puppets in plays, on television and in movies.

Kermit the frog

9

Puppets can look like people, animals, monsters or other things.

Finger Puppets

A finger puppet fits on one finger.

Sometimes fingers can be made *into* puppets.

These finger puppets were made with a pen.

Hand Puppets

A hand puppet fits over a hand.

These hand puppets have heads
and hands.
Their bodies are made from fabric.

The puppeteers wear the puppets on their hands.
They move their hands and fingers to make the puppets move.

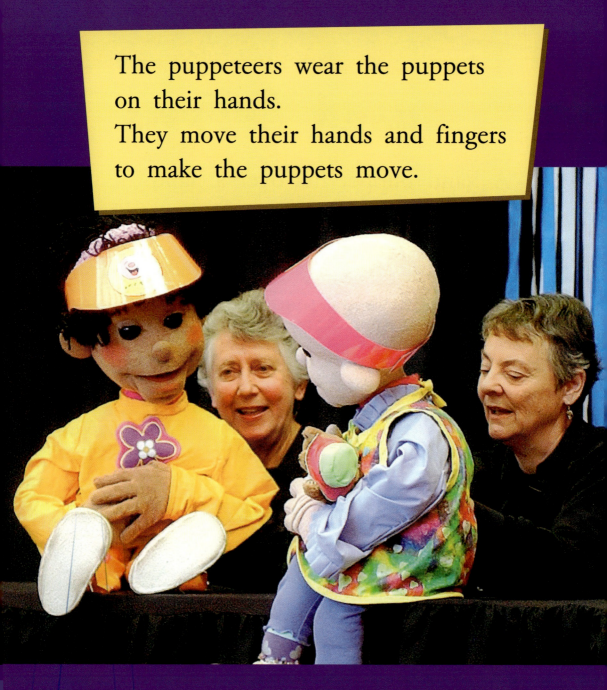

This hand puppet
has a mouth that moves.
The puppeteer opens and shuts his hand
to make the mouth move.

Stick Puppets

A stick puppet has a stick inside it.
Sometimes the puppet's head
is at the end of the stick.

The puppeteer holds onto the stick
with one hand.

This stick puppet has rods on its hands. The puppeteer lifts and pulls the rods to make the puppet's hands move.

String Puppets

A string puppet has lots of strings on it. The strings go up to some sticks that the puppeteer holds.

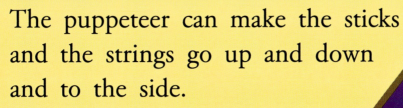

The puppeteer can make the sticks
and the strings go up and down
and to the side.
This moves the puppet.

19

Shadow Puppets

A shadow puppet has sticks on it. The puppeteer moves the sticks to make the puppet move.

20

A shadow puppet is held behind a **screen**.
When a light shines on the puppet,
its shadow falls on the screen.

People sit in front of the screen to watch the puppet play.

Make a Puppet

You will need:

- a small paper plate
- paints or felt pens
- a straw
- glue.

1. Paint a face and some hair
on your paper plate.
Let it dry.

2. Glue the straw
to the back of the plate.

Glossary

actors   people who play other people in plays

play   a story told by actors on a stage

puppeteers people who make puppets move around

screen   thin paper or cloth that you look at to watch a shadow puppet play

Index